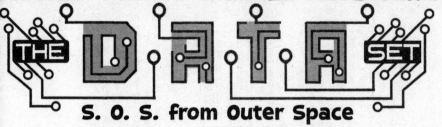

DANGER! ACTION! TROUBLE! ADVENTURE!

THE DATA SET

S. O. S. from Outer Space

By Ada Hopper

Illustrated by Rafael Kirschner of Glass House Graphics

LITTLE SIMON

New York London Toronto Sydney New Delhi

This book is a work of fiction. Any references to historical events, real people, or real places are used fictitiously. Other names, characters, places, and events are products of the author's imagination, and any resemblance to actual events or places or persons, living or dead, is entirely coincidental.

LITTLE SIMON

An imprint of Simon & Schuster Children's Publishing Division
1230 Avenue of the Americas, New York, New York 10020
First Little Simon paperback edition March 2022
Copyright © 2022 by Simon & Schuster, Inc.
Also available in a Little Simon hardcover edition
All rights reserved, including the right of reproduction in whole or in part in any form.
LITTLE SIMON is a registered trademark of Simon & Schuster, Inc., and associated colophon is a trademark of Simon & Schuster, Inc.
For information about special discounts for bulk purchases, please contact Simon & Schuster Special Sales at 1-866-506-1949 or business@simonandschuster.com.
The Simon & Schuster Speakers Bureau can bring authors to your live event. For more information or to book an event contact the Simon & Schuster Speakers Bureau at 1-866-248-3049 or visit our website at www.simonspeakers.com.
Designed by Jocahn Kwon
Manufactured in the United States of America 0222 MTN
10 9 8 7 6 5 4 3 2 1
This book has been cataloged with the Library of Congress.
ISBN 978-1-6659-0297-7 (hc)
ISBN 978-1-6659-0296-0 (pbk)
ISBN 978-1-6659-0298-4 (ebook)

CONTENTS

Chapter 1

A Familiar Message

"He fakes left, he passes right! Rodriguez is in position. He shoots and—GOOOOOAL!" Cesar cried out the winning score for his favorite soccer team.

Gabe, Laura, and Olive grinned as Cesar did a victory lap around the tree house. The four second-grade whiz kids—otherwise known as the DATA Set—were together listening to the Global Soccer Cup finals on Laura's super-powered radio. Cesar was a huge soccer fan, and thanks to his photographic

memory, he knew each player's statistics by heart. The game was being broadcast live all the way from Argentina.

"Congrats, Cesar!" Gabe said. "Your team won!"

"Huzzah!" Cesar spun around, showing off his autographed Rodriguez soccer jersey. "I wore my lucky jersey. They had good Cesar vibes coming at them from halfway around the world!"

"You know, speaking of 'around the world,'" Olive said, glancing over at Laura, "your international radio is really cool. I feel like I'm at the game in Argentina!"

"Thanks!" Laura said, grinning. "I've been tinkering with it lately. The signals are coming in stronger than ever."

Laura turned the dial to the right, and suddenly a woman was singing a lovely French ballad. With another twist, the radio tuned into an Australian comedy festival.

"Can you try tuning in to the International Space Station?" Gabe asked eagerly.

Olive giggled. "I think that might be a little *too* far, don't you?" she asked.

But to Olive's surprise, her friends shook their heads.

"No, Laura's radio does reach outer space," Cesar said matter-of-factly.

"Actually, come to think of it, it's *been* to outer space too," Gabe added.

Olive's eyes grew wide with surprise. "Really?"

Laura nodded. "It's a long story." She turned the knobs as she tried to find the radio frequency of

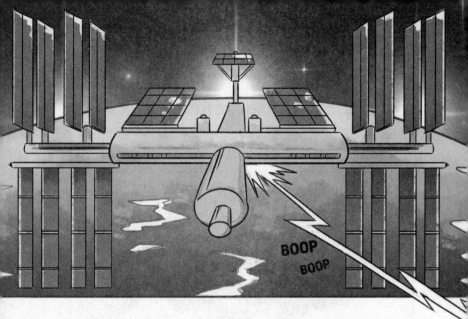

the International Space Station. "I don't know if I can tap into NASA's signals," she said. "But this . . . might . . . just . . . do it."

Laura adjusted a control. Static sizzled and popped over the speakers. Then suddenly, a familiar sound came through.

Boop-boop. Beep-boop-beep.

"I don't believe it," Laura said softly.

"Why? What is it?" Olive asked.

"It's a message . . . from someone we know!"

BLURP

BRRT

BEEP BOOP

BEEP

Chapter 2

Best Alien Friends

"We have to get to Dr. Bunsen's lab!" Laura exclaimed.

She grabbed her radio, and the DATA Set sped down the tree house elevator.

"We got a surprise message," Laura cried, getting on her bike. "From Fave!"

"Who's Fave?" Olive called after her.

"Laura's alien best friend," Cesar said.

Olive blinked, unsure she had heard correctly. "Laura has an *alien* best friend?"

"She sure does," said Cesar, wiggling his arms to imitate the tiny alien. "Four arms? Big eyes? We *must* have told you about him."

"Uh...no." Olive shook her head.

"Oh, I'll explain when we get there," Cesar said. The kids sped over to Bunsen's front lawn, and then Cesar gave Olive a quick debrief.

"So, hold on a minute. Let me get this straight," Olive recapped. "Dr. B invented a machine called the Bunsimmunicator 3000 that could send messages to outer space?"

"Right," said Cesar.

"And an alien named Fave came down to our planet?"

"That is correct." Cesar nodded.

"And when Fave used Laura's radio to call home, his parents came and beamed you up into their spaceship?"

"You're three for three," Cesar confirmed.

"How come you never told me you were abducted by aliens?" Olive asked.

"I thought we had," Cesar admitted. "But time travel, alien abduction, and robots—when you're a part of the DATA Set, it all starts to blend together."

"Dr. B!" Laura shouted as they ran into the lab. Bunsen was nowhere to be found, but they could hear clanging coming down the hallway.

"This way," Gabe declared, leading the team to the back door. They found Dr. Bunsen in his backyard in a giant metal cylinder . . . that was four stories high! The doctor was up on a platform, tightening a bolt to the side of a huge spaceship.

"Dr. B, what is going on here?" Gabe asked in disbelief.

But Dr. Bunsen couldn't hear him.

"Earth to Dr. B!" Olive shouted.

The doctor was wearing headphones and singing along to a rock song. *"I guess there is just me to blame. We're leaving ground on the Bunsen Countdown!"*

"Oh no, how in the world are we going to get his attention?" Laura asked.

That's when
Cesar spotted
a long, hollow
pipe that was
attached to Dr.
B's platform. "I
have an idea!"
Cesar ran over to
it, put his mouth
up against
the opening,
and bellowed,
"GOOOOOOOAAAAALLLLL!"

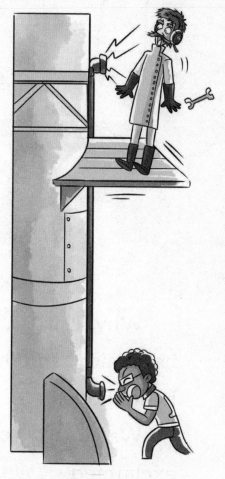

The vibrations shook all the way
up and made Dr. Bunsen jump.

"Why, if it isn't the DATA Set!" he said, finally removing his headphones.

"We need your help!" Laura exclaimed. "We got a message from outer space. Our old friend, Fave, is trying to reach us!"

"Oh, what excellent timing!"
The doctor slid down the pole.
"Because with my USS Bunsen
Blaster, *you* will be able to reach
him!"

Chapter 3

S.O.S. from Outer Space

"This rocket is incredible!" Gabe said as Dr. Bunsen gave them a tour inside the USS Bunsen Blaster.

The doctor smiled proudly. "As you can see, it has autopilot settings." He tapped a few buttons on a control panel and a digital map of the universe popped up.

"Welcome aboard the USS Bunsen Blaster," a friendly automated voice announced. "Which galaxy would you like to visit today?"

The kids didn't have time to answer because Bunsen had so much to show them.

"This new spaceship also has four passenger pods," the doctor chatted on, "with gravity comfort selections, hydrosonic showers, and space food machines!"

"That. Is. So. Cool!" Cesar shouted as he picked a cosmic sundae from the menu. Instantly, a bowl of crystalized blue ice cream came out of the food machine.

"Who knew blue space ice cream was so good?" Cesar shoveled ice cream into his mouth. "Ack! I've got space brain freeze!" Cesar sat down to take a break, but the rest of the DATA Set had so many questions.

"Hang on," Olive said, studying the digital map. "There are galaxies way beyond the Milky Way showing up here. It would take us thousands of years to reach that far!"

"Ah, yes, I did come across that problem before." The doctor nodded. "Luckily, I solved the equation for warp speed velocity.

Otherwise, I wouldn't have been due to return until"— he checked his watch—"thirty-three thousand four hundred and twenty-two years from now."

"What? You never told us you'd been to space!" Cesar cried.

"Well, after I invented the Bunsimmunicator 3000, I figured— why not go into space myself?" Dr. B explained. "My missions were during school hours. That's the beauty of warp speed velocity. You can travel anywhere in the universe and still be home in time for dinner."

"And you never invited us?" Cesar gasped. "That would have been the best field trip ever!"

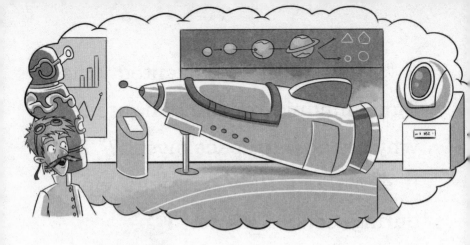

"What happened to your other rockets?" Laura asked.

"Decommissioned," the doctor said, adjusting his goggles. "Or, most recently, put on display in the Museum of Human Artifacts just outside the Kuiper Belt."

Gabe's eyes lit up. "So you've visited other planets? Jupiter? Saturn? Uranus?"

"Yes, yes, and Uran-yes!" replied the doctor.

"How about other galaxies?" asked Cesar. "I memorized all the ones listed in my space encyclopedia. The farthest one we know of is GN-z11."

"I'm afraid I'm not allowed there anymore," Dr. Bunsen whispered. "Turns out beatboxing is quite frowned upon in some parts of the universe."

"But can we really use your rocket to reach Fave?" Laura asked.

"Oh yes, right! The mysterious message!" Dr. Bunsen clapped his hands. "Let's plug in your radio to my Bunsimmunicator 3000 and see what Fave says!"

The DATA Set followed the doctor to the main part of his lab. Laura hooked up her radio so Dr. B's machine could translate the message.

Boop-boop. Beep-boop-beep.

The Bunsimmunicator whirred.

"S.O.S. FROM OUTER SPACE," it translated.

"Oh no, S.O.S!" Laura gasped. "That stands for trouble. Fave needs our help!"

Chapter 4

Space Training

"Then it's time to suit up!" Dr. Bunsen exclaimed. He led them to a display case containing several futuristic space suits. Soon, the DATA Set looked like real astronauts.

"Now you're dressed for the mission," Dr. B declared. "But you must also train for the job. For that, we will need to use my new anti-gravity chamber."

Dr. Bunsen ushered the kids into a glass chamber with several large, circular discs on the floor.

"Please select an anti-grav pad and we'll begin," the doctor instructed.

"I hope this doesn't make me sick," Olive said as she stepped onto her circle.

"Nah, it's just like floating," Cesar said with a wave. "How bad could it beeeeeeeeeee?"

With a *whoosh*, the children were lifted up and suspended in midair.

"Whoa!" exclaimed Gabe. "It's like we're flying!"

"This is awesome!" Laura pretended to swim through the air. "Olive, you should try some of your gymnastics moves."

Olive nodded then flipped over five times. "That's a quintuple twist!"

"Oh man, I can't look," Cesar said with his hand over his mouth. "Zero gravity . . . is worse than I thought. That blue ice cream might come back up."

"Do not fear! Bunsen is here!" Dr. Bunsen restored the gravity in the chamber and the DATA Set floated back down.

Cesar let out a large burp. "Whoa, that was a close call," he panted. "I'm not looking forward to take off. At. All."

That's when Gabe looked around at the team. "Where's your suit, Dr. B? Aren't you going to come with us?" he asked.

"I would love to, my dear boy," the doctor said. "But the weight limit of the USS Bunsen Blaster is quite specific. I'm afraid there's no room for me on this mission."

"You mean we'll

be in outer space by ourselves?"
Laura asked.

"Yes indeed, but weirder things
have happened, wouldn't you say?
And you'll have me on standby if
anything comes up," said Dr. B.

"Okay, but I just need to know
one thing before we go: How

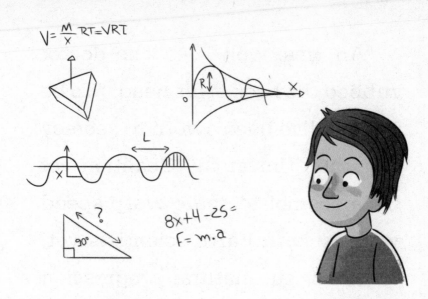

$V = \frac{M}{X}$ $RT = VRT$

$8x + 4 - 25 =$
$F = m.a$

does warp speed velocity exactly work?" Gabe asked curiously as he looked at Dr. Bunsen's notes. "I've read Einstein's theory of special relativity. As we approach the speed of light, wouldn't time slow down for us but move forward for everyone else?"

"Ah, yes, well . . ." The doctor rubbed the back of his head. "To be honest, I've been sworn to secrecy by the Universal Coalition of Galaxies not to share warp speed velocity with Earth scientists yet. To honor the natural progression of technology and all."

"Okay, but our parents think we're having a sleepover in our tree house," Laura pointed out. "How long will we have?"

"You have exactly twenty-four hours." Dr. Bunsen spread his arms wide. "As long as you can complete your mission and be back by then, all will be fine in the universe.

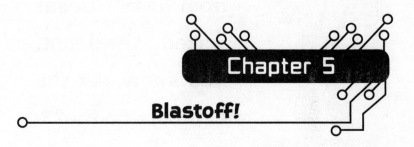

Chapter 5

Blastoff!

The DATA Set watched in awe as Dr. Bunsen removed the ceiling of the rocket ship to uncover the central launch pad.

"Dr. B, this is seriously SO cool!" Gabe whistled. "I know you've built a lot of incredible inventions, but this rocket is . . . out of this world!"

"Wait, but can we actually blast off from here?" Cesar asked. "And not, you know, set the neighbors on fire?"

"Most definitely!" exclaimed the doctor. "Heat-proofing, vibration-cancellation, and sound-buffering, have all been accounted for. But the one tricky bit has always been the bright lights from the blaster. If things are not timed perfectly, the flash from the blastoff will be visible due to the high warp speed. . . ."

The doctor's voice trailed off as he stared into space. But then, just as quickly, he snapped out of it. "No matter! It's never been an issue before."

The DATA Set all froze for a moment, smiling at one another nervously.

"Umm, I guess flashing lights aren't that big of a deal . . . right?" Olive said first.

"Yeah, we'll be fine!" cried Gabe. "I've been waiting to go to outer space since I was five!"

"And I've wanted another blue cosmic sundae since I learned it existed five minutes ago!" added Cesar.

"Great! Roger that. But remember, we need to help Fave," Laura reminded them. "That's our real mission." Gabe and the rest of the DATA Set nodded.

With that, Dr. Bunsen strapped the kids into their space pods. Then he connected Laura's radio to the control panel so it could detect Fave's space signal.

Instantly, a flight path popped up on the screen. Fave's signal had come from a galaxy far beyond the Milky Way, on an uncharted planet.

"All set, my fearless travelers?" Dr. Bunsen asked.

"Yes, sir! Ready for blastoff!" Gabe and the gang gave a big thumbs-up.

Dr. B sealed the rocket door with a big *THUNK*. Then the countdown began.

"Ten, nine, eight," his voice echoed over the intercom. "Seven, six, five, four, three, two, one . . . BLASTOFF!"

With a massive shudder, the USS Bunsen Blaster thundered off the launchpad, hurtling through the atmosphere.

"I-I-I-I C-C-CAN'T F-F-F-EEL M-M-MY F-F-F-ACE!" Cesar's teeth clattered together.

"This was a bad idea!" Olive shouted above the deafening noise.

"Just hang on!" Laura cried. "I'M SURE ... WE'RE ALMOST ... THERE!"

The kids held onto their chairs for what felt like an eternity until everything went quiet. The rocket boosters shut off. The shaking stopped. And the DATA Set slowly opened their eyes to find the USS Bunsen Blaster floating through space, surrounded by countless stars.

Chapter 6

Across the Cosmos

"Come in, DATA Set! Do you read me?" Dr. Bunsen's voice crackled over the intercom.

"Yes, we're fine, Dr. B," Gabe answered back.

"We're better than fine—we're great!" exclaimed Laura. "Outer space is amazing!"

The kids gazed out the window in absolute wonder. The Earth was so far away that it looked like a tiny, swirled marble. Ahead of them stretched millions of stars, twinkling against the deep blackness of space.

"Huzzah!" cheered the doctor. "Could anyone see the flash of the big blastoff?" Olive asked.

"Oh yes, it was quite the spectacular light show," Dr. B said. "But hopefully, not too many people saw. Now, when you're ready, press the big blue button. That will put the ship into auto warp speed mode, so you can reach Fave's planet faster."

Gabe did as Dr. B said, and the rocket lurched forward. The distant stars began streaking by like long beams of light.

"We're on our way!" Gabe confirmed.

DING DONG!

Just then, a doorbell chimed in the background by Dr. Bunsen.

"The doorbell?" the doctor asked curiously. "But I never get visitors."

"Is everything okay, Dr. B?" asked Gabe.

"Yes, yes, but it looks like I've got to go. You know how to reach me, but for now, good luck, my young DATA Set!"

When the call ended, Olive touched the screen to look at the map.

"How long will take to reach Fave's planet?" Olive asked.

The rocket computer hummed to life. "You will reach your destination in five hours and thirty-seven minutes," announced the friendly voice.

"Thank goodness. It sounds like we've got a little time," Cesar said. He unbuckled himself and floated out of his chair. "I say, let's get this rocket party started!"

The kids high-fived each other. For the next few hours, they would be able to enjoy the special features of the USS Bunsen Blaster.

They used the food machine to make yummy space s'mores. They played zero-gravity ping-pong and even had a flipping contest. They also caught a few space z's in the sleep pods so they would be fresh and alert when they finally reached Fave's home.

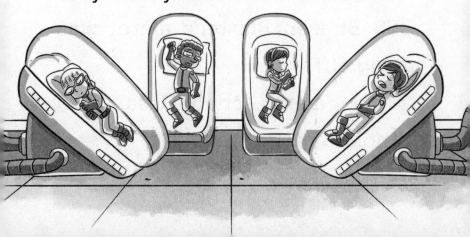

BRRRT! BRRRT! BRRRT!

The DATA Set jolted awake. The USS Bunsen Blaster's alarm was going off!

"Red alert!" cried Cesar. "All hands to battle stations!"

"We're not under attack," Laura said, rubbing her eyes. "That's the landing sequence alarm. Look! We're here!"

The friends huddled around the window. Out in the distance they could see a rainbow-colored planet with spirals of orbiting rings.

"Strap in!" Gabe said. "This might get bumpy!"

The USS Bunsen Blaster shook and shuddered as the rocket thrusters turned on. The colorful planet grew closer until . . .

FWOOOOSHHH! They safely landed!

They quickly unbuckled their

seatbelts, grabbed their helmets, and opened the door. A retractable ramp lowered down to the ground, and the DATA Set carefully stepped out into a bright, glowing light.

And when the kids looked up, they were face-to-face with the perfect surprise.

Chapter 7

Greetings, Earthlings!

"Oh, Fave!" cried Laura. "It's really you!"

The little four-armed alien was waiting for them at the bottom of the ramp.

Laura rushed forward to hug her friend. "I can't believe we found you!"

While Laura and Fave reunited, the rest of the DATA Set marveled at everything around them—Fave's planet was out of this world!

Arches made of colorful crystal stretched high, weaving in and out of sleek futuristic buildings with shape-shifting windows. The USS Bunsen Blaster had landed on a glowing spaceport that changed from yellow to orange to green. Aliens of all shapes and sizes were whizzing by in silver space

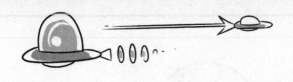

saucers. And high above, the DATA Set could make out the sparkling rings and twelve moons orbiting the planet.

"Your home planet is amazing, Fave!" said Gabe.

"Oh Gabe, Fave can't understand our language," Cesar reminded him.

But the little alien smiled big. Fave held up a glowing orange orb gemstone in his hands. It looked just like the one Fave's parents had used when they came to Earth. "Don't worry, I have my translator orb. Welcome to the Poly Chrome Galaxy!"

"Thank you, Fave! But we got your message," Laura said. "Are you in danger?"

"Danger?" Fave tilted his head. "What do you mean?"

"Your message said 'S.O.S,'" Laura insisted. "That's a call for help for humans on Earth."

"Oh dear," Fave said. "On my planet, S.O.S means *Sleppp Orrrghtzzz Slortzup.*"

Laura giggled. "We don't know what that means, Fave."

"It means 'Wish you were here,'" explained Fave. "I had wanted you to come visit, but I had no idea you thought I was in danger!"

"Well, this is good news!" Olive jumped up and down. "Since

everything is okay, we have twelve whole hours to explore!"

Fave looked at Olive curiously. "I do not remember you. Are you a DATA Set?"

"This is Olive," Laura said. "And yes, she is definitely a member of the DATA Set."

Then Olive happily shook all four of Fave's hands.

"Well, as I think you earthlings would say—huzzah!" Fave exclaimed. "Follow me!"

The little alien led the DATA Set through the bustling spaceport. And soon, they came to a silver and green saucer with one seat.

"I don't think we can all squeeze in there," said Cesar. "I ate *a lot* of galactic space ice cream."

"Not to worry!" Fave cried. Then he pressed a button and the little ship expanded into an even bigger saucer.

After everyone was buckled in, Fave smiled. "Our next stop is the Poly Chrome Meteor Park!"

Chapter 8

The Poly Chrome Meteor Park

Fave's space saucer whizzed over his home planet's terrain. Gabe, Laura, Cesar, and Olive were speechless as they pressed their noses against the glass. Everything here looked so different.

Upside-down mountains rose tall, mist surrounding their peaks.

Every so often, the mist would release a rainstorm of sparkling dust that powdered the ground. The moons that orbited high above shone bright colors that created

rainbow moonbeams across the sky. Laura gazed down as they skimmed over a field of alien plants.

"Laura, look!" Olive pointed ahead.

A soft glow on the horizon became brighter and brighter. Fave sailed around one final mountain . . . and Meteor Park came into full view.

"You weren't kidding!" Cesar gasped. "It's actually a *meteor* park!"

The friends couldn't believe their eyes. The amusement park was built on dozens of floating meteors! Jet-booster roller coasters

zoomed from space rock to space rock, while hundreds of aliens of all shapes and sizes waited in line on floating staircases. At the center was a spectacular glowing orb pulsing every color imaginable in one epic light show.

"Is that what I think it is?" Cesar pointed toward a giant arena. Aliens kicked flaming balls into shimmering nets while a massive crowd watched.

"That is my favorite sport called alexipix," Fave said.

"Well, on Earth, it's called . . . SOCCER!" cried Cesar.

One of the aliens kicked his fiery ball into the net.

"GOOOOOOOOALLLLLL!!!!" cried Cesar.

"FWWWEEEERRPPP!" roared the crowd.

Right then, Fave flew his ship down into a docking bay. "We're here!" he announced.

"Let's go! Let's go! Let's go!" the kids cheered. They were ready for an epic intergalactic amusement park day!

Gabe and Olive decided to hit the roller coasters first. "I-I-I-I C-C-C-C-AN'T F-F-F-FEEL M-M-M-MY B-B-B-B-BRAIN!" Gabe shouted as they skyrocketed around a twisting infinity loop.

"Hey Fave, check this out!" Laura was playing a ring toss game where the ring would disappear into a small space portal and reappear a hundred yards away. "I think I just won a space teddy bear!"

Meanwhile, Cesar headed for the snack bar. "Why doesn't this exist on Earth?!" he said as he gobbled up rainbow slime. "This is my new favorite dessert EVER!"

After that, they crammed into a supersonic photo booth to snap a group photo. Cesar even won a game of Whack-a-Space-Slug! His prize was a light-up replica of the

giant space ball at the center of the Meteor Park. Even though it was tiny, it was powerful enough to create an  awesome light show in the night sky.

"I think I need a break," Laura said, exhausted.

"Yeah, and my stomach's growling," Gabe added.

"Then I know exactly where we can go!" Fave cried.

Chapter 9

Home Sweet Space Home

After a short flight over the upside-down mountains, Fave safely landed the saucer and his parents greeted the DATA Set in front of their mushroom-shaped house.

"Hello to the DATA Set—it's great to see you again," Fave's mom spoke through her orb translator.

"It's good to see you, too!" Laura smiled.

"You are just in time for dinner," Fave's dad said. "Please, come in."

Inside their home, everything was sleek, smooth, and bright

white. White seats. White lights. White walls. But each time a surface was touched, a ripple of rainbow colors exploded across the blank canvas.

"It feels like we're inside of a painting," marveled Olive.

At the table, a wide spread of strange-looking leaves and spiky vines were laid out on platters for dinner.

"Um, is it okay that the food is . . . wiggling?" asked Gabe.

"Do not worry. These are what you would call fruits and

vegetables on our planet," Fave's mom assured them. "Please enjoy."

Gabe, Laura, Cesar, and Olive each sampled a teeny-tiny bite.

Fave watched as Laura's eyes lit up. "You're kidding me. This is delicious!" she cried.

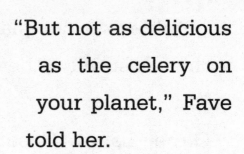

"But not as delicious as the celery on your planet," Fave told her.

Olive giggled. "We'll agree to disagree on that one." Then she took a huge bite of a squishy purple vine.

The DATA Set munched and happily chatted with Fave's family. The kids were all surprised to learn that some things were the same here as on Earth. Fave had to go to school every day. And he even had to help with chores. The only difference was that they had futuristic cleaning supplies the kids had never seen before.

Then, after dinner, they headed to Fave's room.

"Wow, you have so many awards!" Laura admired Fave's collection. "You must be really smart."

"No, it is you who is really smart," Fave told them. "I've told everyone I know about the DATA Set who saved me from being stuck on their planet."

The DATA Set laughed. "Yeah, we're glad we were able to get you back home," Laura said. "If only we didn't live so far away."

"I know," agreed Fave. "But at least now we can talk on the radio I built." Fave showed her a replica of her international radio.

"You made a radio just like mine?" Laura whispered.

"Yes, a subspace radio!" Fave grinned. "It's how I reached you! Now we can keep in touch every day."

Laura hugged her friend. "It's perfect, Fave."

Just then, a high-pitched whine screeched out from Fave's radio. When he adjusted the knob, a familiar frantic voice came through.

"DATA Set? Are you there, DATA Set?"

It was Dr. Bunsen!

"S.O.S. from Earth!"

S.O.S. FROM EARTH!

Chapter 10
S.O.S. from Earth!

"What's wrong, Dr. B?" the DATA Set yelled through the radio.

"Oh, thank goodness I got through to you!" The doctor breathed a sigh of relief. "You must come home quickly. There's been a small . . . development."

"What do you mean?" asked Laura.

"Well," the doctor's voice crackled. "The light show from your blastoff attracted more attention than expected. The neighbors are asking questions, a crowd has formed, and I'm concerned the Universal Coalition of Galaxies might step in if we don't bring you back immediately."

"Okay, say no more. We'll get back as soon as we can," Gabe said.

Quickly, the DATA Set hopped aboard Fave's saucer and returned to the spaceport.

"I guess this is goodbye again," Laura said sadly to her friend.

Fave handed Laura one of the photos they took at Meteor Park. "But now we will have a lot to talk about over our radios."

Laura nodded. "We sure will!"

The DATA Set boarded the USS Bunsen Blaster and prepared for blastoff.

"I just hope I won't feel like throwing up again," Cesar said with a gulp.

Then the countdown began until . . . *FWOOOOOM!* The rocket blasted off the launchpad. "N-N-N-NOPE!" Cesar's teeth clattered again. "J-J-J-JUST L-L-L-IKE B-B-B-BEFORE!"

Then soon, everything quieted down and the DATA Set sailed across the cosmos. Exhausted from their interstellar adventure, they slept most of the way back until a familiar warning alarm blared as they reached Earth's atmosphere.

"I see the crowd!" Laura exclaimed as they approached Dr. Bunsen's landing pad. "Oh, my gosh, even the mayor is there!"

"With government agents," Gabe added. He recognized the three men from the first time they had met Fave. "This doesn't look good."

Fortunately, the crowd was gathered in front of Dr. B's mansion, so the rocket was able to land without a sound, shielded by his noise-buffering force field. But just as before, the light from the rocket boosters was visible.

"There it is again!" cried the crowd. "The mysterious light show!"

"Just *what* is going on, Dr. Bunsen?" the mayor asked.

"Well, uh, you see, the thing is . . . ," Dr. B stammered.

"It's just our science project light

show!" Cesar declared. He and the DATA Set stepped through the front door of Dr. B's mansion, still wearing their space suits. "We're predicting what an intergalactic space party would look like," he said. "With this!"

Cesar held up the light orb he had

won at Meteor Park.

The crowd *ooohhhed* and *ahhhed* as the lights from Cesar's orb filled the sky. It looked just like the flashing  lights from the rocket blastoff and landing!

"So, this whole time we've been going berserk over a school science project?" the mayor said in disbelief.

The doctor nodded uneasily. He wasn't sure if he was off the hook, but any questions could wait thanks to the DATA Set's awesome timing. The kids came and saved the day—just like always.

And luckily, at least for tonight, any weird happenings in Newtonburg would all be forgotten, thanks to an epic adventure with an old friend, an awesome light show, and a poly chromatic souvenir from the greatest place in all the galaxies.

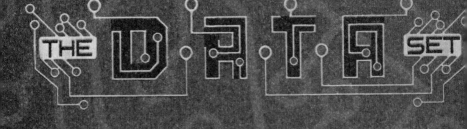

FOR MORE DANGER! ACTION! TROUBLE! ADVENTURE!

Check out all the previous books